JIM E

INDEPENDENCE

WAR IN IRELAND, 20–21 NOVEMBER 1920

SCHOLASTIC

PROLOGUE

21 NOVEMBER 1920
CROKE PARK, DUBLIN

We made our way in through the turnstiles, and headed for Hill 60, a grassy hill that had been built at the railway end of Croke Park to give spectators a chance to get a better view. We found ourselves a spot about halfway up the hill.

More and more spectators poured in through the turnstiles, climbing the hill and filling up the terraces. By the time the match was ready to begin, it looked like there were at least five thousand people inside Croke Park. A huge crowd.

After the usual announcements and introductions, the two teams came out onto the pitch to be met with a huge roar – the Dubs in their sky-blue shirts and Tipp in their white jerseys with a green diagonal sash.

"Dubs! Dubs!" and "Jackeens!" we shouted, which were the Dublin rallying cries. The Tipperary supporters responded with a chorus of, "Tipp! Tipp!"

For the first time since meeting Michael Collins and the other IRA members, I was able to think about something other than what I'd heard. I stopped thinking about anything other than the match. This was going to be a clash of giants, the two best football teams in Ireland!

The game started brilliantly, the players showing their skills as they kicked, caught and passed at a speed that made your heart stop. The game had only been going on for a few minutes when we heard a shot ring out. The sound of it cut through the noise of the crowd and everyone fell silent.

The players stopped, bewildered and unsure of what was happening. Then suddenly we saw a force of Tans rush in from the turnstiles end, rifles levelled, firing into the crowd and at the players.

There was panic. The crowd yelling and rushing to try and get away.

"Make for the wall!" shouted Sean, pointing to the wall that bordered the canal end. I could see that the people nearest to the wall were already climbing it to get out, but as they reached the top we heard gunfire from outside the stadium and they fell back down. They were being shot at!

"The Tans are outside, on the canal bridge!" shouted Con. "There's no way out that way!"

Bullets were thudding around us.

"Get down!" shouted Sean. He grabbed me and threw me on the ground. "Crawl towards the main gate!"

I started to crawl. As I did, I glanced towards the pitch. Some of the players had managed to run towards the terraces, but others were lying on the grass. Some moved, some didn't. Con and Rory were crawling alongside us. Con got to his feet.

"For goodness sake, there are women and children here!" he shouted at the Tans.

The next second, I saw him stumble back and then fall. Blood was spreading out over his white shirt from beneath his jacket.

"Da!" screamed Rory.

Uncle Sean dived for his brother, getting to Con just before Rory.

"He's alive," Sean shouted at Rory. "He's just wounded."

He looked pretty badly wounded to me. He was unconscious, his eyes closed and his mouth open. His face was deathly white.

"Liam, get Rory to safety," said Sean. "I'll look after Con."

"But—" I began, feeling helpless. "I don't know what to do!"

"Just go!" shouted Sean. "Keep Rory with you. Make for home. I'll see you back there."

Rory was crying, his body heaving with great sobs as he looked at his father lying on the ground.

"Come on, Rory," I said. I took him by the arm, but he shook me off.

"I'm staying with my da!" he burst out.

"No, you're not," Sean shouted at him. "Your da will be all right. Go! Go with Liam and do what he tells you. Go now!"

CHAPTER

"Pay attention, Liam! You'll drop that bag if you're not careful, and there's eggs in it!"

"Sorry, Aunt Mary," I said.

I was supposed to be helping my aunt carry the shopping, but all I could think of was the big match the next day. Tomorrow, Sunday, was the day of the Gaelic Athletic Association, the GAA, football final between Dublin and Tipperary at Croke Park. I couldn't wait because I had tickets for it, along with my uncles Sean and Con, and Con's son, my younger cousin, Rory.

My name's Liam Donnelly. I'm eleven years old and I live in Kilmainham in Dublin with my Uncle Sean and my Aunt Mary. On Saturday mornings Aunt Mary ropes me into helping her with the shopping, which means I end up carrying the heaviest bags. I don't mind because Aunt Mary lets me choose a sweet from McGinty's Toffee Shop as payment, so it's a fair deal.

My da, Patrick Donnelly, was killed in the Easter Rising of 1916, and my ma, Katharine, died in the flu epidemic of 1918 that followed the Great War. Uncle Sean and Aunt Mary's own daughters, my little cousins Maeve and Nuala, died during the same flu epidemic. They were just three years old. Over fifty million people around the world died in that flu epidemic of 1918, a quarter of a million in Ireland and Britain alone, but the death of my ma was what I remembered. Uncle Sean and Aunt Mary kept a shrine to Maeve and Nuala in their bedroom. I kept a shrine for my ma in my heart.

It was after my ma and my little cousins died that Uncle Sean and Aunt Mary took me in and gave me a home. They've been as good as any parent could ever be to me, but I still think about my poor ma and da and wonder what life would be like for me if they hadn't died.

Anyway, this Saturday morning we'd nearly finished our shopping. We were just coming out of Derry's, the butchers, when we were stopped by two Tans, who pointed their rifles at us.

"What you got in your bag?" demanded one with a scowl.

Black and Tans was the name we'd given to the thugs from England who'd been sent to join with the men of the Royal Irish Constabulary (RIC). The first Tans arrived in Ireland just last year, when the British realized they were losing the war against the Irish Republican Army (IRA) and they needed more men. Most of these thugs had been soldiers in the British army during the Great War, though some were men who'd been let out of British jails if they signed up to join the Tans. They still act like they're soldiers or criminals, even though they're supposed to be part of the RIC.

They're known as the Black and Tans because of the uniforms they wear. The RIC didn't have enough proper uniforms for them when they first arrived, so they wear British army khaki trousers and RIC bottle-green tunics, which are almost black, although Uncle Sean says the "Black" comes from the colour of their hearts, because they are the nastiest and most violent creatures who ever walked the earth.

When our war started in 1919, it was Irishmen fighting for freedom from British rule. Irish volunteers in everyday clothes, using whatever weapons they could find, often old rifles that had been used to shoot rabbits on farms. On the British side was the Royal Irish Constabulary; mostly Irishmen themselves, but paid by the British Government, who believed that Ireland should still be part of the British Empire. Backing the RIC was the British army – one of the most powerful armies in the world. The British army had just won a war against Germany. The Irish volunteers wanted us to have the freedom to rule ourselves. They wanted a government of Irish people, voted for by Irish people, to make the decisions on how Ireland should be run, instead of all the decisions being made in the British Parliament in London.

My Uncle Sean says the British thought that, with

their better weapons and their military training, they could put down the Irish volunteers quickly, just as they had in the uprising of 1916 when my da was killed.

But the Irish volunteers weren't put down. Instead they got better organized and became an actual army – the Irish Republican Army. In the countryside, they ambushed the British soldiers and the RIC, then stole away. In the towns and cities, they shot at the British soldiers and then vanished into the streets. Their success was mostly thanks to Michael Collins. He's the military commander of the IRA. Collins is a genius and a hero. He's always coming up with ways to defeat the British by any means. One of his best tactics is arming small groups with pistols and directing them to make surprise attacks and escape quickly before the enemy can go after them. The IRA are our own people; they know the country and the streets of where we live like the backs of their hands, so they can disappear fast.

Because the British think that Michael Collins is so dangerous, they're offering a reward of ten thousand pounds to anyone who can capture him, dead or alive. Ten thousand pounds! That's more money than most people will see in their lifetime! Or in lots of lifetimes around here. But the Irish people are loyal to Collins and no one has ever even thought of betraying him. My Uncle Sean says freedom is worth more than any amount of money. And if anyone did betray Michael Collins, that traitor would be killed before he was able to collect the reward.

Most Irish people would rather get into real trouble with the Black and Tans than hand in one of our own. Of all the British forces fighting us, soldiers and police, the Black and Tans are the worst. Everyone I know thinks they are evil and get their fun from bullying women and children. Like they were doing now, with Aunt Mary and me.

When Aunt Mary didn't answer, just glared back at them, the Tan repeated his question in a nastier tone of voice.

"I said: what you got in your bag?" he growled.

"Shopping," replied Aunt Mary, looking at the pair of them coldly.

"Open it!" he snarled, and he poked the end of his rifle hard into Aunt Mary's shopping bag, making her stumble backwards.

"Leave her alone!" I shouted at him.

The other one swung his free hand, hitting me round the head with such a clout that I saw stars and tears came to my eyes.

"He's lying!" snarled the one who'd hit me. "Shoot the boy!"

CHAPTER

"What's going on here?"

The voice was that of a British army officer. I could tell he was an officer by the posh way he spoke. The Tans looked uneasily at one another. The one who'd hit me was big and muscular with a red face. The other was short and thin, with a face like a rat. His two little rat eyes were darting left and right, as if looking for an escape.

"We're searching two suspected troublemakers, sir," grunted the big one who'd hit me.

"We think they might have weapons hidden in the shopping bag," added rat-face.

The officer appeared from behind me and looked at the two Tans. From his khaki uniform and his peaked cap, and especially from the amount of brass buttons and stuff he wore on his shoulders, I could tell he was quite important. No one seems to know who's supposed to be in charge of the British side during this war, the British Army or the Royal Irish Constabulary. Mostly it's reckoned to be the army, but the RIC insist the army are just there to back them up. One thing's for sure, both the army and the RIC are supposed to be above the Tans – although you wouldn't think so from the way the Tans swagger and throw their weight about.

From the grim expression on the officer's face and the way he glared at the two Tans, I could tell he was angry. He turned to Aunt Mary.

"My apologies for the rough way these men were treating you and the boy, madam," he said. "But, as they have raised the matter, I have to ask you: are you carrying any weapons in that bag?"

"No," said Aunt Mary. She held out the open

shopping bag for the officer to look in.

"A piece of meat and some potatoes," said the officer. "Thank you, madam."

"She wouldn't open it when we asked!" said one of the Tans defensively.

The officer ignored him. "Once again, madam, my apologies for the way you were treated," he said politely to Aunt Mary and me.

Aunt Mary gave him a small but unsmiling nod, then gestured for me and her to move on. As we did, I heard the officer telling off the two Tans.

"We are fighting a war," said the officer. "That does not include terrorizing women and children."

"But, sir, the way these Irish fight – they use women and children!" protested one of the Tans.

"Yes, sir. Everyone knows the men get them to smuggle their weapons!" added the other. "They could have had guns in them bags!"

"But they did not!" snapped the officer. "Now get about your business!"

Aunt Mary and I continued on our way home.

"Thanks be to God, this war will soon be over and we'll be rid of them and their like," she said.

"We were lucky the British officer came along," I commented.

Aunt Mary looked at me sharply.

"Don't trust any of them!" she snapped. "Remember, they're the ones that killed your poor da!"

Uncle Sean was out in the backyard, mending his bicycle when we got home. He stopped as soon as he saw the angry frown on Aunt Mary's face.

"Did something happen?" he asked.

"The Tans," I told him. "They wanted to search the shopping. And one hit me on the head."

Uncle Sean's expression darkened.

"Where are they?" he demanded, wiping his oily hands on a cloth. "I'll teach them some manners!"

"No, Sean," said Aunt Mary.

"A British army officer came along and stopped them," I said. "He told them off."

"Huh! The British army!" Sean snorted. "We wouldn't have this trouble if the British army weren't here in the first place!" He gave a small nod of satisfaction. "Anyway, it won't be for much longer. They'll be driven out soon enough, I promise you!"

CHAPTER

Later that afternoon, Uncle Sean headed off on his bicycle to the field where the Dublin team were getting ready for tomorrow's GAA final. He was great shakes as a footballer himself, though to my mind his best game was hurling. Hurling is the fastest game there's ever been, and much more skilful than football. In Gaelic football you have a round ball that you pass to one another, either by throwing it or kicking it, and you have to get it in the net of the goal for three points, or over the crossbar and between the upright posts for one point.

Hurling has the same scoring system, three points for a goal and one for over the bar, but it's played with a much smaller and harder ball called a sliotar. You use a hurley, which is a wooden stick with a flat blade at the end to catch and hit the sliotar.

My da and Uncle Con played hurling as well, but they weren't as good as Uncle Sean. I've seen Uncle Sean hit a goal from the halfway line, driving the sliotar so hard and fast no one could see it moving, let alone stop it.

Uncle Con arrived in his taxi just after six o'clock. He often came round in the evenings and I was always glad to see him. He's the youngest of the three brothers – my da, Patrick, was the oldest. Con's the liveliest, always ready with a joke, no matter how hard things are. In that way he's very different from Uncle Sean, who always seems to have the weight of the world on his shoulders.

"Good evening to you, Mary!" he greeted my aunt. "I've come to see if the young fella would like a spin in the taxi."

"Yes!" I burst out.

My two uncles owned the taxi between them and they took turns to drive it, one of them doing the night driving, while the other carried fares during the day. They took turns, two days about, so today Uncle Con was doing the day and the evening shift.

"I'm not sure about that," said Aunt Mary doubtfully. "I don't want Liam being out late."

"Ah, come on, Mary," said Uncle Con with a smile. "It's a Saturday night and he hasn't got to get up for school tomorrow."

"There's morning Mass to go to," she said.

"And the game afterwards. Come on, what's the harm?"

"Please, Aunt Mary!" I begged.

She hesitated, then nodded.

"Very well. But take care of him. Don't get him into any trouble."

"Ah, Mary, would I do a thing like that?" Uncle Con said grinning.

We went out to the taxi and I climbed in the back, just like a real fare-paying passenger.

"Where are we going, Con?" I asked.

"It's a surprise," he said. "Something special."

"Isn't Rory coming with us?" I asked.

He shook his head.

"Rory's a bit young for this particular surprise," he said, which made me wonder what it could be.

I didn't pay much attention to where we were headed as he drove, because I was too busy talking about tomorrow's match. I wondered if Con might take us to the field where the Dublin team were practising, but instead he took us into the city, driving down backstreets. He avoided the main streets where the British soldiers and the Tans tended to be stationed, stopping and questioning ordinary people as they went about their business. Finally, Con pulled to a halt outside a big house in Lower Gardiner Street.

"Here we are," he said.

"What's here?" I asked, puzzled. It was just a big old house; it didn't look much like a surprise. Not an interesting or exciting one, anyway.

"There's some fellas in there you ought to meet," he said.

"Who?" I asked.

Con grinned.

"That's the surprise," he said. Then his face became serious. "But listen, Liam, this is very special and top secret. I want you to promise to never say a word about who's here, or anything that happens. Promise?"

"I promise," I said.

As I followed Uncle Con down the path towards the house, I wondered what on earth we would find that was so secret. I reckoned it must be to do with the IRA. Uncle Con had taken part in the Easter Rising, along with my da, but while my da had been killed, Con had been taken prisoner and put in jail.

I followed Con to the back of the house. He made for a door and knocked on it three times, then whispered, "Con."

There was the sound of a key turning in the lock, then the door opened and Con ushered me into a kitchen. The man who'd opened the door locked it again.

He was an ordinary-looking man of about thirty in shirtsleeves and a woolly grey jumper, but what drew my eyes was the pistol he wore in a holster hanging from his shoulder.

"Evening, Tom," said Con cheerfully.

"Con," the man said with a nod, but his eyes were on me, regarding me with suspicion.

"This is my nephew, Liam," said Con. "My brother Pat's son. I thought it'd be good for him to meet some of the boys after the meeting. Will you keep an eye on him?"

Tom smiled. "Of course."

He gestured to a chair at the small wooden table. "Set yourself down, boy, and make yourself comfortable."

"The usual room at the back?" asked Con.

Tom nodded.

"Now you just stay here with Tom, Liam," said Con. "I'll be back shortly."

With that, Con left the kitchen and headed down a passageway before turning off it and disappearing down another.

Judging by the size of the kitchen and the number of passageways, this was a big house. I wondered who lived here? Someone important, I guessed. I sat down at the table.

"So, you're Pat Donnelly's son," said Tom, sitting down on a chair beside the back door.

"I am," I replied.

Tom nodded, his face sympathetic.

"Pat was a great man," he said. "I was with him at the rising in '16. Along with Con. Con and me were at Frongoch together, with most of the men in that room there."

"Frongoch?" I said, puzzled.

"Has Con never told you about Frongoch?" he said, surprised.

I shook my head.

"He never says much to me about the rising. I think – because my da was killed there – he reckons it will upset me."

Tom shook his head.

"Your da was a hero," he said. "And that fact should make you proud, not upset you."

"I know," I told him. "And I know he was shot by the British. I know about the battle at the General Post Office where he died."

"Fighting for Irish freedom, God rest him," said Tom sadly. Then he looked at me and grinned. "But Frongoch was very different. It was a prison we were dumped in, but it was more like a university for us, with that many Irish volunteers all packed into one place, everyone teaching everyone else about guns and bombs and the best way to conduct an ambush. The Big Man himself was there with us. Sure, didn't he teach us."

The Big Man was what most Irish people called Michael Collins, the leader of the IRA. Because he really is a big man, very tall and powerfully built. Eamon de Valera, the President of the IRA, is just as tall, but he's much thinner, so he's known as the Long Fella. But I'm told he isn't called that to his face.

"Where was Frongoch?" I asked.

"Wales," he said. "It was a British prisoner-of-war camp for German prisoners during their war, but there weren't enough Germans there, so they got rid of the few they had and put us in it instead. Two thousand of us." He smiled at the memory. "Sure, it was actually pretty good. Yes, we missed our families, but we were all pals together in one place."

There was a tap at the back door and Tom was immediately alert. He leaped to his feet, his hand going to his pistol. But he calmed when he heard a voice outside say quietly: "Tom. It's Jack. I just want a quick word."

"I'll come out," called Tom. He smiled at me. "Jack's my brother. We'll take our business outside. I won't be long."

Tom opened the door and went out into the yard at the back, pulling the door shut after him.

I realized I needed to go to the toilet and I wondered where it was. In our terraced house it was in an outhouse in the backyard, but I hadn't seen an outhouse near the door we'd come in by. I guessed there must be another door that led outside to it, so I went out into the passage that Con had walked down. As I passed a door I heard voices from behind it. The words I heard stopped me in my tracks.

"We'll kill all of them in the one swoop," said a voice I recognized instantly. I'd heard him speak at rallies, addressing crowds in the streets, urging them to fight for Irish freedom. It was the voice of Michael Collins himself.

CHAPTER

I stood rooted to the spot, shocked and fascinated, as Collins continued.

"We'll destroy the whole Cairo Gang and all those other agents and informers. We'll get all fifty of them in one go."

Then another man spoke. "No, Michael," he said. "I've studied the list and there's not enough evidence against fifteen of these men."

"All those men are agents for the British," insisted Collins.

"There's sure evidence against thirty-five of them," said the other man. "Against these other fifteen, it's just gossip and hearsay. We don't kill people without evidence, Michael. This is about justice."

I heard a chair scrape as someone in the room stood up. Worried someone would come out and find me listening, I hurried along the passageway in search of the toilet. They were talking about killing spies and informers – I didn't want them to think I was one!

I found a door to the outside. Pushing it open, I caught the smell of the toilet coming from a small outhouse. While I was in there I tried to come to terms with what I'd heard. They were talking about killing people! And my Uncle Con was one of them! Was he a killer?

I did my business then returned to the house and walked down the passage. This time the door was open and the men were coming out. Con saw me and frowned. "I told you to stay in the kitchen, Liam," he said.

"I went to the toilet," I explained.

Then the figure of Michael Collins himself appeared behind Con.

"Is this the young fella you were telling me about, Con?" he said.

"It is indeed, Michael. This is my nephew, Liam."

"Pat's boy." Collins nodded. He smiled and held out his hand to me. "It's a pleasure to meet you, as it was an honour to know your father. He was a great man and a true patriot. If we'd had a few hundred more like him at the rising, Ireland would be free today."

"It's an honour to meet you, Mr Collins," I said, and it was. Here I was, shaking hands with the legendary Michael Collins, the man who held the might of the British at bay.

"Call me Michael," said Collins. He turned and grinned at Con. "Me and your Uncle Con once shared a cell, so we think of ourselves as family."

Another man appeared behind Collins. I recognized his voice as the man who'd opposed Collins when they were talking about how many people to kill.

"So, Con, some of the boys are off to Vaughan's," said the man. "Can they trouble you for a ride? Yours is the one taxi in Dublin where we can be sure we won't be betrayed to the Brits."

"Of course, Cathal." Con nodded, and I realized

the man was Cathal Brugha, Minister for Defence in the Irish Government. Not that the British recognized our government. As far as they were concerned, it was all the IRA, and illegal. But as far as we Irish were concerned, we'd voted for the people who'd stood for the Sinn Féin party at the recent election. They'd won and so we considered them to be our proper government. An Irish Government voted for by Irish people, whether the British liked it or not.

"You're not coming yourself, Cathal?" asked another man.

"No, Peadar," Cathal replied. I thought the man that had asked must be Peadar Clancy, another IRA hero. "I have things to do this evening, preparing for the storm that will come tomorrow."

He nodded politely to us, and left.

Con led the way along the passage, with me, Michael Collins, Peadar Clancy and two other men behind him. From the conversations going on between the men I worked out that these other two were Dick McKee and Piaras Béaslaí. It struck me that if Con's taxi was stopped by soldiers tonight, all the top men in the IRA would be captured in one go.

CHAPTER

We crammed into Con's taxi and drove to Vaughan's, a grand hotel in Parnell Square, where the men got drinks for themselves and a lemonade for me. As I sipped at my drink I couldn't help but keep glancing at the doors, scared the British army would suddenly burst in. But Collins and the others didn't seem worried. They appeared relaxed as they sat in the bar and talked, mainly about tomorrow's game between Dublin and Tipp.

"Dublin will win," predicted Clancy confidently.

"But they'll have to keep a sharp eye on Michael Hogan, he's some fair player."

"So, how did you get on with Tom?" Con asked me.

"Good," I said. "He told me about Frongoch."

"Ha, Frongoch!" laughed Collins. "Good times! Do you remember that canteen worker there who taught us Welsh?"

"Johnny Roberts from Bala," said Con.

"That was him. A fine young man. Educated."

The barman appeared with a tray of more drinks, which he set down on the table.

"There's a man called Conor Clune, just arrived from County Clare, to meet you," he told us. "He's in the restaurant."

Béaslaí stood up. "I'll go and see him. Clune's a good man."

The men were just starting to chat again, when the hotel porter hurried in. When they saw the concerned expression on his face they were immediately alert.

"Trouble?" asked Collins.

"Maybe," the porter said. "One of the guests just made a late-night telephone call and then left the hotel. I'm thinking he might have contacted the soldiery."

Collins stood up. "It's a shame to leave a table of drinks, lads, but it's time for us to go." He turned to Con. "Thanks for the ride. We'll see you in the morning."

"You will indeed, Michael," said Con. "Come on, Liam."

In the taxi on the way home, I wanted to ask Con about the killings that I'd overheard the men planning. But if I did, he'd know I'd listened at the door, and I was scared he'd be angry with me.

When we arrived home, I could see at once that Aunt Mary and Uncle Sean were upset.

"You promised you wouldn't keep him out late!" said Aunt Mary.

"Ah, Mary, 'tis just the one night. And it's a Saturday," said Con defensively.

"Where were you?" demanded Sean.

"I took him to meet some of the boys," said Con. "He needs to know who our true friends are if he's going to become involved in the struggle."

"He's not going to get involved!" burst out Mary. "For goodness sake, haven't we had enough death in this family!" She pulled a handkerchief from her pocket, put it to her eyes and ran out of the room.

"He's already involved!" Con shouted after her. "He's Irish!"

Sean stepped towards his younger brother, his fists clenched.

"You'll not speak to my wife in that manner, Con," he growled. "And certainly not in this house."

Con looked like he was about to disagree, but instead he dropped his head.

"I'm sorry. Sean, I'll go up and apologize," he said.

"You'll not," said Sean firmly. "You'll trouble her no more tonight."

Con nodded. "Then please tell her I apologized for what I said."

"It's not what you said, it's what you did!" said Sean angrily. "Taking Liam to a place like that. You should have talked to me or Mary first!"

Con gave a heavy sigh.

"You're right, Sean, as always," he admitted. "I should have asked you first." But then he looked defiantly at his brother. "But you'd have said no. And Liam needs to know what our struggle is about! Our cause!"

"He knows!" retorted Sean. "His father, our much-loved brother, died for the cause. And I've never forgotten that and neither has Liam. And neither has Mary."

Con glared back at Sean and for a moment I thought they might even come to blows. But then Con sighed and nodded.

"I was wrong to do what I did," he said. He headed for the front door. When he got there, he turned to me and gave me an awkward grin.

"See you at the match tomorrow, Liam," he said, before leaving.

CHAPTER

When I went to bed that night, my mind was whirling with all the things I'd heard and seen that evening. Michael Collins. Dick McKee. Peadar Clancy. Tomorrow they were going to kill thirty-five men and I was sure my own Uncle Con was going to be one of the killers.

How were they feeling tonight, knowing what they were going to be doing tomorrow? I didn't understand how they could sit and chat and laugh in the bar at Vaughan's, knowing what lay ahead. If I was in their position, I'd be sick with fear and nerves.

There was a tap at my door, then Uncle Sean appeared.

"Are you asleep, Liam?"

"No," I said.

Uncle Sean came in and sat down on the chair beside my bed.

"I'm sorry about that row tonight, with Con. It wasn't your fault, but your aunt and I were worried about what could have happened to you. These are dangerous times."

He fell into a thoughtful silence. I didn't say anything, wondering whether he was about to tell me off for going with Con in the taxi. But instead, he said: "The time of the rising, before your da died, he asked me and Con to go with him to the General Post Office to take it over. Con said yes, but I said no. I had the girls, you see. They were just one-year-olds at the time. The way I saw it, I needed to stay alive for them, provide for them." His head lowered and he said in a voice filled with tears, "After the flu came, I questioned if I'd done the right thing."

He was talking about Maeve and Nuala, my twin

cousins. Two years later they died in the flu epidemic that also took my ma.

"If there'd been more of us ready to fight that Easter, maybe the British would have been beaten and we'd have our own free island now," said Uncle Sean. "But I didn't go. And your da died, alongside so many others."

His face clouded and he fell into an unhappy silence, before adding: "I can still remember the executions of the leaders of the rising. Patrick Pearse, Tom Clarke, Sean MacDermot, Joseph Plunkett, Eamonn Ceant, Thomas MacDonaugh and James Connolly…

"It's haunted me ever since, Liam. Not going with your da. But tomorrow, I'm going to be making up for that."

"You're going with Con and Michael Collins and the others?" I asked, shocked.

He looked at me and I saw a flash of anger cross his face.

"Did Con tell you about it?" he demanded.

"No," I said. "I heard them talking about it when I went to the toilet."

"'Talking about it'?" he queried.

"I heard Michael Collins say they were going to kill fifty people. The Cairo Gang, he called them."

Sean nodded. "The Cairo Gang are the most dangerous of all the British spy rings operating in Ireland."

"Why are they called the Cairo Gang?" I asked.

"Because they meet at the Cairo Cafe in Grafton Street and because many of them served in Cairo in Egypt during the Great War. Thanks to them, we've lost many good people, killed or imprisoned, and there's a danger that they're spreading their spy networks so we'll lose even more. We need to put an end to them, otherwise we'll never win this war."

"And you're going along with Uncle Con and the others tomorrow?" I asked.

Uncle Sean nodded. "I'm going to be the driver."

The sound of heavy banging on the front door woke me up. I got out of bed and stumbled onto the landing. Uncle Sean and Aunt Mary were already heading downstairs in their dressing gowns. Uncle Sean was holding a thick stick.

"Is it the Tans?' I asked anxiously.

Sean whispered for me to stay back.

Outside, the loud banging on the front door continued. Then we heard Con's voice. "Sean! Mary! It's Con!"

Sean undid the bolts and chain on the door and opened it. Uncle Con fell into the passage.

"What's going on?" demanded Sean as he shut the door.

"McKee and Clancy have been arrested and taken to Dublin Castle!"

I swallowed nervously. Dublin Castle was the regional seat of the British Government in Ireland.

"What?" asked Sean.

"They were snatched in Sean Fitzpatrick's bar in Gloucester Street," said Con. "Someone in the bar must have betrayed them. The Brits also lifted the man who came to Vaughan's to meet the boys, Conor Clune. They grabbed him just after we left. He's been taken to Dublin Castle, too! What do we do about tomorrow?"

"Anyone else taken?" asked Sean.

"Not as far as I've heard," said Con. "But if they talk…"

"McKee and Clancy won't," said Sean grimly. "What about this other man, Conor Clune?"

"He wasn't at the meeting," said Con. "He only came to Vaughan's afterwards. He knows nothing."

"So, we go ahead as planned," said Sean.

CHAPTER

When I woke up the next morning Uncle Sean was gone. I asked Aunt Mary where he was, but she just said that he and Con had gone off in the taxi. Even though she didn't say any more I could tell she was worried and knew what Sean and Con were going to do. Normally, she made breakfast with ease, frying the bacon and eggs and hash while putting on the kettle for tea and slicing bread. But today she dropped an egg on the kitchen floor and nicked her finger with the bread knife. I wondered if Uncle Sean had told her he'd talked to me about what was planned, but as she didn't say anything, I didn't want to add to her worries by bringing it up.

I'd wanted to say something to Uncle Sean before he left, to wish him luck and urge him to come home safely. I wanted to tell him how grateful I was to him for the way he'd looked after me as if I was his own son. But being woken up in the middle of the night by Con's loud knocking meant that I'd slept in longer than I'd intended.

I went through to our outhouse to use the toilet and heard our neighbours talking in their backyard. They were discussing Dick McKee and Peadar Clancy's arrests. It sounded like there was a price on their heads, and they'd been betrayed. How far had the betrayal gone? Had McKee and Clancy been tortured to make them talk? The Tans were capable of all manner of evil and torturing prisoners wouldn't trouble their conscience. I wondered if Sean and Con had been named? My heart hammered in my chest at the thought. I took a deep breath and tried to calm down. If they had been named then the Tans would have been round to arrest them. The fact that Sean and Con had gone off OK meant that the Brits didn't know what was planned for this morning. They didn't know the plan to destroy the Cairo Gang and their spies and informers.

Aunt Mary hardly spoke during breakfast, just put my plate down in front of me and told me to eat up. I noticed that she didn't have anything herself, and guessed she was too worried to be able to eat. I was worried too, but for me eating was a good distraction.

After I'd finished, Aunt Mary told me we were going to early Mass so I'd be back in time for the match.

I didn't say anything, but I worried whether Sean and Con would make it back at all, let alone in time for the match. They were going on a dangerous mission, up against hardened British soldiers and agents who'd survived through the Great War. How would they succeed? Would Sean and Con have to face all thirty-five men themselves, or just some of them?

I was being daft. They would just be going after one or two of them. Other men would be going after the others. That was the IRA way, small groups of twos or threes who appeared, carried out an ambush, then disappeared again, able to melt back quickly into the local alleys. There'd been a lot of men the previous evening at the house in Lower Gardiner Street, taking their orders. Con taking the orders for him and Sean.

Would they be with another man? Quite likely. Sean had said he was driving. So that would mean Con and someone else would be doing the shooting.

How would Con feel when he pulled the trigger? Scared? Guilty? Or would he feel it was just revenge for his brother, my da?

Aunt Mary made me put on my best clothes and we made our way to church for Mass. When we got there, I looked for my cousin Rory and my Aunt Kathleen, but I couldn't see them anywhere. This struck me as very strange. I guessed they weren't here because of what Con was up to. Aunt Kathleen was always a very nervous woman and if she knew what Con was going to be doing today, she would have been even more nervous than usual.

I noticed that although Aunt Mary went through all the motions of the service, her attention wasn't on it so much as usual. Except that when she prayed she seemed to be praying harder and longer than I'd seen her pray before. I knew she was praying for Sean and Con to come home safely.

CHAPTER

After Mass, instead of going straight home, we went to Uncle Con's house to collect my cousin Rory.

"As he's going to the match with you this afternoon, he can join us for dinner first," said Aunt Mary.

Uncle Con, Aunt Kathleen and Rory only lived a few streets away from us. When we went together to a match, me and Uncle Sean usually called for Con and Rory on the way. We always caught a bus to Croke Park rather than take the taxi, because traffic was always busy on match days, and I knew that Sean and Con didn't like leaving their precious taxi unattended in a crowd of strangers.

We arrived at Uncle Con's house and found Rory playing outside, kicking a ball against a wall.

"Liam!" he called excitedly when he saw me. "It's going to be a great game this afternoon!" He threw the ball to me and I caught it. "Come on! I'll be the Dubs and you be Tipp!"

"Yes, you play out here with Rory," said Aunt Mary. "I won't be a minute. I just need to talk to your Aunt Kathleen."

Aunt Mary went into the house and shut the door. I kicked the ball back to Rory. He caught it and bounced it before kicking it back to me.

"I don't think Mammy's well," he said. "She's been crying all morning."

I didn't know what to say. Con must have said something to Aunt Mary, asking her to keep an eye on Aunt Kathleen. Kathleen must know what Con was doing this morning and be worried sick that he might get arrested. If he was arrested, this time he'd surely be hanged.

Rory and I carried on playing football. We were

lucky that the house was in a dead-end street with no passing traffic, so we had the whole road to play in. We marked a goal with our jackets against one wall. I made sure we picked a wall with no windows. Years ago, I'd been playing football with Uncle Con and I'd accidentally kicked a ball through a window. The man who lived in the house had come out swinging a cudgel and threatened to beat me with it. I was lucky Con had been able to calm him down.

After a long while, the door of the house opened and Mary came out.

"Put your coats on, boys," she said. "You're coming home with us, Rory."

The fact that she didn't tell us off for balling up our best jackets and using them as goalposts showed her mind was on other things.

"How's Mammy?" asked Rory. "Is she all right?"

"She is," said Mary. "She's having a bit of a sleep at the moment, so we won't disturb her. She'll be fine when you come home after the match."

Rory and I picked up our jackets and put them on, then Rory picked up the ball. We began to walk towards our house. I looked at Aunt Mary, wondering if she'd say anything more, but she just kept walking, her face a grim mask.

It was when we got to our street that her expression changed. Her eyes opened wide and she broke into a run. As I followed her, I saw what she'd seen. The front door of our house was open. Who was in there? Were my uncles home already? Or was it the Tans?

CHAPTER

Aunt Mary burst into the house with me and Rory close behind.

"Sean!" she cried out.

Both my uncles were in the kitchen, Con sitting at the table and Sean standing over him, dabbing at his arm with a cloth. The cloth was red. Then I saw the basin on the table, filled with bloody water. Con had been hurt.

"Da!" cried Rory, and he ran to his father.

"I'm all right, son," said Con. "Just a scratch."

Aunt Mary pushed Sean to one side and examined the bleeding gash on Con's arm.

"It'll need to be stitched," she said. "I'll do it. Liam, get the iodine from the cupboard."

I went to the cupboard where Aunt Mary kept bottles of medicines and creams and other useful things.

"Iodine?" said Con unhappily. "That stuff stings something terrible!"

"It'll stop that cut getting infected," Mary snapped back, taking her needles and thread from the table drawer.

"Light a candle, Sean, so I can sterilize the needle," she ordered.

Sean nodded and picked up a candle in a saucer, which was always kept in the kitchen. He brought it to the table and lit it.

"Now go and tell Kathleen that Con's made it back. He's had a slight graze, but I'm dealing with it." She hesitated, then added: "You'd better bring her over here. She'll want to see Con herself, to believe it. But don't bring her back until I've sewed his arm. I don't want her wailing all over the place while I'm doing it. Give me half an hour."

"Right." Sean nodded.

"You can take the boys with you, as well," said Mary. "They can play kick-about in the street."

"I want to stay with Da," protested Rory.

"You'll go and come back with your mammy when I'm done," said Mary firmly. "Now be off with you."

We were turning to leave, when Mary suddenly moved over to Sean and pulled him to her, hugging him hard.

"Never frighten me like that again, Sean Donnelly," she said. "Or I swear, I'll kill you myself."

Sean hugged her tightly and kissed her.

"Hey, you two, there's a man bleeding to death here!" complained Con.

"No, you are not!" snapped Mary. But she let go of Sean and moved back to the table. "You said yourself, it's just a scratch. Now stop your complaining and grit your teeth, like the big strong man you think you are."

"Come on, lads," said Uncle Sean. "We'll leave your aunt to her doctoring."

As we left the house, we heard Uncle Con give a roar of pain.

"That'll be the iodine," said Sean with a smile. "Let's

move on before she starts with the needle and thread."

We walked along the street, questions bubbling in my head.

"Did it—" I stopped and shot a look at Rory to make sure he couldn't hear us before finishing. "Did it go all right? Apart from Con getting hurt."

He gave a short nod.

"It did. At least, our bit. One for Ireland." Then he gave me a warning glance not to say anything more in front of Rory.

We walked on, and I wondered what had happened? How many had they killed? And how had Con got that gash in his arm?

CHAPTER

Rory and I waited outside while Uncle Sean went into the house to tell Aunt Kathleen what had happened to Con. Rory and I heard her let out a shriek, but it was cut short. I guessed that Sean had put his hand over her mouth so the noise didn't attract the attention of the neighbours.

Rory and I didn't play football this time, we just waited. Finally, Sean came out with Kathleen. Her face was dead white and her eyes red raw from crying. She had her coat pulled tight and she walked so fast that

Rory, Sean and I had difficulty keeping up with her.

"Aunt Mary told you to keep her back for half an hour," I said to Sean.

"That's all very well for your aunt to say, but it'd be like trying to hold back a raging bull," said Sean ruefully. "She wants to see Con for herself."

Aunt Mary was still sewing up Con's arm when we arrived back. As soon as she saw Con, Aunt Kathleen let out a cry and threw herself at him, wrapping her arms around him. Con gave a yelp.

"Get off him, Kathleen!" barked Mary. "I'm not finished sewing his arm yet!"

The sharp tone of authority in her voice did what Sean couldn't do. It made Kathleen stop and step away from Con.

"I'm all right, my love," Con assured her. "Mary's nearly finished."

"If you want to do something, you can put the kettle on and make us all a cup of tea," said Mary.

Kathleen did as she was told, filling the kettle and putting it on the stove. Mary put the final stitch in Con's arm then tied the thread off before cutting it. I saw the sweat and flash of pain on Con's face as Mary did this, but he gritted his teeth and didn't cry out, obviously not wanting to upset Kathleen. Mary put more iodine on Con's arm, then bandaged it.

"There," she said.

"Thank you, Mary," said Con. "A doctor couldn't have done a better job."

"No, he couldn't," said Mary. "And a doctor wouldn't prepare your dinner for you afterwards." Turning to me, she said, "Liam, go and get some potatoes and start peeling them."

When the food was on the table and grace was said, we fell on it. Mary had got her appetite back, and Con and Sean wolfed down the meat and potatoes and cabbage. The only one who seemed not to have an appetite was Kathleen. She picked at the food and in the end she offered her plate to Rory, who finished it. Uncle Con looked at the clock on the mantle.

"Just in time," he said. "We've got a match to get to."

"You're not going to the game!" said Kathleen, shocked.

"Of course we are!" said Con. "We've got tickets and we promised the boys."

"Let them go," Mary said to her. "God's given them back to us. They deserve the break."

We all put on our jackets, with Con wincing as he pulled his sleeve over his injured arm. We caught the bus, and I began to hear mutterings about murders from the other passengers. Those who talked kept their voices low and glanced around to check on who might be listening.

How many people have been murdered? I wondered. Michael Collins said he had a list of fifty people, and the other man, Cathal Brugha, had tried to get him to cut it down to thirty-five. Had all thirty-five of the Cairo Gang and their informers been killed? I looked at Con and Sean and wondered how many of the targets they had attacked.

I looked out of the windows and noticed that there were more soldiers, Tans and police on the streets than usual, even for a match day. There was a nervousness about them as they watched the crowds heading for the stadium. Usually, they carried their rifles slung over their shoulders, but today they held them cradled in their hands, barrels pointing as if they were ready to fire.

We got off the bus along with the other passengers. The pavements were jammed with men making their way to Croke Park. I could see that the huge number of people, four or five thousand, was making the soldiers even more nervous. They stood in groups, silent and grim, rifles ready.

"They're on edge," muttered Con. "It only needs a bad look at one of them and they'll start."

"Keep your gaze away from them, boys," said Sean to me and Rory. "Don't give them cause to do anything. And slow down. Don't walk too fast."

We walked, our eyes turned towards one another, not looking at the uniformed men. I was aware of the soldiers glaring at us, suspicious and fearful. Suddenly we found our way barred by four Tans, who pointed their rifles at us. There was no mistaking the hatred in their faces.

"Where do you think you're going?" one of them barked.

"To the match," said Sean.

"Got tickets for it, have you?" he sneered. "You Irish are liars, the whole lot of you."

Sean didn't reply. Instead, he pulled out the tickets

for the game and held them out for the Tan to see. I expected the Tan to take them from him, maybe screw them up and throw them in the gutter, but he didn't. The Tan scowled.

"We'll have our revenge for what your lot did this morning," he snarled.

He stepped back and gestured for the other Tans to do the same. They did, and we moved forward, following Sean. All the time I was expecting them to hit out at us with their rifles, but they let us pass.

"We'll be all right once we're inside the stadium," said Sean. "We'll be safe there."

The nearer we got to Croke Park the more soldiers and Tans we saw. It was as if they were scanning the crowd, looking for particular people. I glanced nervously at Sean and Con, worried that someone might have seen them when they were on their mission this morning.

CHAPTER

We were just arriving at the stadium, when we heard a voice behind us calling: "Sean! Con! Hold hard, lads!"

Although Sean had said for us to keep moving, he stopped and turned. A fellow I'd met just a couple of times before with Sean was hurrying towards us. I remembered him as Brian Dee, a car mechanic who'd worked on the taxi once or twice. Brian looked upset and nervous.

"It's not looking good for this afternoon, lads," he said. "There's talk the Tans will be taking some kind of revenge for what happened this morning."

"Why? What happened this morning?" asked Con, pretending ignorance.

Brian stared at him.

"Sure, haven't you heard? They reckon twenty Brits were shot by the IRA!" He looked nervously about to make sure no uniformed officers were within hearing, then, in a frightened whisper, he told us what he'd heard.

"Three shot in Upper Pembroke Street, another two on Upper Mount Street and one on Lower Mount Street. More shot dead in Lower Baggot Street, Morehampton Road and Gresham's Hotel. It's a massacre! The Tans will be after blood, that's for sure!" He pulled out his ticket for the match. "So I'm looking to sell my ticket for the game."

"Oh, come on, we'll be safe inside Croke Park," said Con.

"I wouldn't be so sure," said Brian. "I've just come along Clonliffe Road and we were held up by a load of soldiers. And there's a convoy of police and Tans moving towards Croke Park from the canal end. There's going to be trouble, lads." He fluttered his ticket in his hands. "So, if you want another ticket. . ."

Sean shook his head.

"Thanks, Brian, but we've already got ours," he said.

Brian nodded, then moved off to find someone else to sell his ticket to.

"D'you reckon he's right?" I asked Sean and Con. "They'll make an attack on us at Croke Park?"

"I wouldn't be surprised at anything those devils do," muttered Sean.

"Maybe we ought to go home," suggested Con. He nodded towards me and Rory. "I'm thinking of the boys."

Sean looked past him and shook his head.

"Take a look," he said. "We'll not be going anywhere."

We turned and looked in the direction he pointed, and saw that soldiers had begun to set up roadblocks across the roads leading towards the stadium. There were also armed soldiers standing on the pavements near the roadblocks.

"What's happening?" asked Rory.

"Either they're there to keep anyone else out, or to keep us in," said Sean.

"Maybe they're expecting more trouble, and that's

what this is about," suggested Con.

"Maybe," said Sean. "I'm sure they won't come into the stadium, so that's the safest place to be. Let's go in and get ourselves a good spot."

CHAPTER

We made our way in through the turnstiles, and headed for Hill 60, a grassy hill that had been built at the railway end of Croke Park to give spectators a chance to get a better view. We found ourselves a spot about halfway up.

More and more spectators poured in through the turnstiles, climbing the hill and filling up the terraces. By the time the match was ready to begin, it looked like there were at least five thousand people inside Croke Park. A huge crowd.

After the usual announcements and introductions, the two teams came out onto the pitch to be met with a huge roar – the Dubs in their sky-blue shirts and Tipp in their white jerseys with a green diagonal sash.

"Dubs! Dubs!" and "Jackeens!" we shouted, which were the Dublin rallying cries. The Tipperary supporters responded with a chorus of, "Tipp! Tipp!"

For the first time since meeting Michael Collins and the other IRA members, I was able to think about something other than what I'd heard. I stopped thinking about anything other than the match. This was going to be a clash of giants, the two best football teams in Ireland!

The game started brilliantly, the players showing their skills as they kicked, caught and passed at a speed that made your heart stop. The game had only been going on for a few minutes when we heard a shot ring out. The sound of it cut through the noise of the crowd and everyone fell silent.

The players stopped, bewildered and unsure of what was happening. Then suddenly we saw a force of Tans rush in from the turnstiles end, rifles levelled, firing into the crowd and at the players.

There was panic. The crowd yelling and rushing to try and get away.

"Make for the wall!" shouted Sean, pointing to the wall that bordered the canal end. I could see that the people nearest to the wall were already climbing it to get out, but as they reached the top we heard gunfire from outside the stadium and they fell back down. They were being shot at!

"The Tans are outside, on the canal bridge!" shouted Con. "There's no way out that way!"

Bullets were thudding around us.

"Get down!" shouted Sean. He grabbed me and threw me on the ground. "Crawl towards the main gate!"

I started to crawl. As I did, I glanced towards the pitch. Some of the players had managed to run towards the terraces, but others were lying on the grass. Some moved, some didn't. Con and Rory were crawling alongside us. Con got to his feet.

"For goodness sake, there are women and children here!" he shouted at the Tans.

The next second, I saw him stumble back and then fall. Blood was spreading out over his white shirt from beneath his jacket.

"Da!" screamed Rory.

Uncle Sean dived for his brother, getting to Con just before Rory.

"He's alive," Sean shouted at Rory. "He's just wounded."

He looked pretty badly wounded to me. He was unconscious, his eyes closed and his mouth open. His face was deathly white.

"Liam, get Rory to safety," said Sean. "I'll look after Con."

"But—" I began, feeling helpless. "I don't know what to do!"

"Just go!" shouted Sean. "Keep Rory with you. Make for home. I'll see you back there."

Rory was crying, his body heaving with great sobs as he looked at his father lying on the ground.

"Come on, Rory," I said. I took him by the arm, but he shook me off.

"I'm staying with my da!" he burst out.

"No, you're not," Sean shouted at him. "Your da will be all right. Go! Go with Liam and do what he tells you. Go now!"

CHAPTER

13

I grabbed Rory by the arm again and dragged him behind me as we ducked down, trying to find a way out. We were both knocked flat by people rushing to get away. I heard screams and yells of pain as other people that had fallen were trodden on by the panicking crowd. If we stayed on the ground like this, we'd get trampled to death.

"Up!" I shouted. I grabbed Rory and hauled us up. Because we were both short, the taller people around us gave us cover from the bullets being fired from the pitch, but only just. As we ran, some people running next to us crumpled and fell, leaving us exposed.

Doing my best to keep us hidden inside the stampeding crowd, we made it to the turnstiles at the entrance. All the time there was shooting from the pitch, with bullets flying around us.

I grabbed Rory and pulled him into the stadium entrance.

"Da..." he began, tears rolling down his face.

"Uncle Sean will look after him. Everything will be fine."

But in my heart, I wasn't so sure. I didn't know if Con was even alive. I was sure that Sean had only told us Con was OK to make certain that Rory left. At least we'd made it to the turnstiles. I was sure that once we were over them and out into the street, we'd be safe. Only we weren't.

I helped Rory clamber over a turnstile, following the crowd into the street ... then I stopped dead. Outside Croke Park, the area was crawling with soldiers, police and Tans, who were trying to hold back the crowds as they poured out. Those at the front turned and tried to get back in to the stadium, away from the rifles pointing at them. But it was no use, the swell of people still trying to get away from the shooting on the pitch meant they couldn't move, and they found themselves forced towards the soldiers.

Suddenly we could hear the terrifying sound of a machine gun opening fire. A chilling *rat-a-tat-rat-a-tat-rat-a-tat* of bullets poured towards the crowd. Along with everyone else I threw myself and Rory to the ground in a desperate bid to avoid being shot.

CHAPTER

The machine-gun fire was coming from an armoured car. Luckily for us, it was aiming above the crowd.

"Stay down!" I ordered Rory, holding him firmly so he wouldn't get up. It was a terrible thing to do, to hide among the injured. But an instinct to survive seemed to take me over as we hid. And then suddenly, the machine gun stopped firing.

"Stay down!" I said again.

We didn't move. Rory was trembling and I lay across him to make sure he stayed down. I was worried that if we got up, they'd start shooting again. I grabbed a chance to look towards the armoured car and the soldiers. The soldiers were keeping their distance from us, but their rifles were still aimed at the crowd.

Slowly, some of the people got to their knees. They faced the soldiers, their hands in the air to show they were unarmed. When the soldiers didn't shoot, and the machine gun didn't start firing again, more people stood up, very slowly, holding their hands high in the air.

"Move forward! Slowly!" shouted an officer. "Keep your hands up!"

Gradually, people began to move forward, shuffling nervously. The soldiers backed away, but kept their guns pointed at us the whole time.

I hauled Rory to his feet. I'd decided we weren't going forward with the crowd. I didn't trust the soldiers. After what I'd seen happen so far today, I thought they might start shooting once they had everyone near to them and standing up.

Keeping a firm hold on Rory, I edged slowly backwards, doing my best to keep behind taller people. Hopefully, if the soldiers did spot us, they would just think we were moving slowly forward along with the rest of the crowd. So long as the soldiers kept their distance, I thought we had a chance.

I kept us moving back, going slowly so as not to trip over the bodies on the ground or bring attention to ourselves, until we reached the wall of the stadium. Then, still keeping a hold on Rory, I edged us close to the wall, aiming to take us round the stadium until I saw a break in the line of soldiers. But as I edged round, I saw there wasn't a break. The soldiers had Croke Park surrounded.

As more and more of the crowd moved forward towards the line of soldiers, it left me and Rory standing on our own against the wall.

"You two!" shouted an English voice. A soldier had spotted us and was heading over, pushing his way through the crowd, his rifle pointed at us.

"Stop there!"

We stopped, and I put my hands up, heart pounding.

"Where are you going?" the soldier demanded.

What to say? If I told him where we lived, some soldiers might follow us there and snoop around.

They might find out about Sean and Con's part in this morning's mission. I needed to lie.

"We're looking for our da," I said. "We got separated from him when we came out of the stadium."

"How old are you?" he growled.

"I'm eleven. He's eight," I said. I tried to make myself look as if I was going to cry, so he'd know I wasn't looking for trouble.

"We only came for the match," I said. "And now we don't know if our da is dead or alive!"

The soldier looked uncomfortable.

"All right," he said. "You can go. Go home. And be thankful for it."

"Yes, sir," I said.

I took hold of Rory's hand and followed the soldier as he led us through the crowd. We reached the line of soldiers and the armoured car with its machine gun. An officer appeared from behind the armoured car and looked sharply at us, and at the soldier.

"What's going on here?" he demanded. "Are they arrested?"

"No, sir," said the soldier. "They can't find their father. I've told them to go home. They're only kids."

The officer stood and studied us suspiciously. Was he going to have us arrested? Or taken to be shot? My throat was so dry and my heart was thumping so loudly that I thought he was sure to notice and have us taken in. But then he shrugged. "Very well. They look harmless. Send them on their way."

CHAPTER

15

We walked back towards my house. I decided we'd stay on the main roads until we got nearer home. I didn't want to use the side streets and alleys and risk coming face to face with a nervous lone soldier ready to take a shot at anyone moving.

Dublin was eerily empty of people. It looked like news of what had happened at Croke Park had spread and people had decided it was safer to stay off the streets. The only exceptions were soldiers who were everywhere, of course. We were stopped a few times and questioned, but each time we told them we were on our way home and they let us pass. Twice we were searched, both times by a patrol of Tans.

We arrived home and opened the door. Aunt Mary and Aunt Kathleen came running from the back kitchen.

"Thanks be to God!" said Aunt Mary, hugging me.

Aunt Kathleen held Rory tight, and then she looked past him towards the open front door.

"Where's your da?" she asked anxiously.

I took a deep breath. I hated to say the words, but I knew they had to be said. "Uncle Con got shot," I said.

"But he's going to be all right," said Rory. "He was just unconscious."

"Uncle Sean stayed with him," I added. "He told us to come home."

Aunt Kathleen began to cry, still holding Rory tightly to her.

Aunt Mary hauled me into the parlour.

"Is that true?" she demanded in an urgent whisper, keeping her voice low so Kathleen wouldn't hear. "Was Con just unconscious?"

"That's what Uncle Sean said," I told her.

"Where was he shot?" she demanded.

I tapped a place high on my chest, just beneath my shoulder.

"It was about here," I said. "But I couldn't see properly because of his jacket, and all the people trying to get away. . ."

"Yes, yes." She nodded, and hugged me to her again. "We heard what happened." Angrily she spat out: "They say it was the Tans."

"It was," I said. "And soldiers."

"What about Sean?"

"He said he'd stay to take care of Con."

She hesitated, then nodded.

"I'll go and find him," she said.

"I wouldn't do that," I said quickly, even though Aunt Mary hated to be disagreed with. "It's dangerous out there. They shot at women and children as well. And I don't know how Aunt Kathleen will cope if you leave her."

She thought it over then nodded again.

"Sean will make his way home once he's taken Con to hospital," she said. "Let's make you a cup of tea."

She let me go and I went back out into the passage.

Rory was there on his own, looking helpless.

"Mammy's gone upstairs," he told us.

"Liam, take Rory into the kitchen and put the kettle on," said Mary.

As I ushered Rory into the kitchen, Mary headed up the stairs to deal with Kathleen.

"Mammy says she doesn't know what we'll do if Da dies," said Rory, his lip trembling and tears coming into his eyes.

"He'll be fine," I assured him. "Uncle Sean will look after him."

But inside I wasn't so sure.

CHAPTER

16

It was a very long afternoon, stretching into the evening, with still no word. A few times Aunt Mary went out into the street to talk to neighbours and see if anyone had heard any more about what was happening, but no one seemed to have any information. It was gone seven o'clock when we heard the street door opening. We were all in the kitchen, sitting silently and worrying, and we all rushed to it.

Uncle Sean stood in the doorway, looking strained, his clothes dark with dried blood.

"Where's Con?" cried Kathleen, rushing past him and out of the door into the street.

"He's in the hospital," said Sean.

"He's alive?" asked Aunt Mary.

"He is." Sean nodded.

"Do you hear that, Kathleen?" called Aunt Mary. "Con's fine!"

"I wouldn't say he's fine," said Sean warily. "He's alive, but the doctors were still operating when I left."

"I have to go to him!" said Kathleen.

"We'll all go," said Mary.

"I'll get changed first," said Sean. He looked down at the dried blood on his clothes. "I'll not go back there looking like this."

Uncle Sean changed his clothes, then he fetched his taxi and drove us to the hospital.

The place was packed with relatives waiting for news of people who'd been brought in, either shot or trampled in the crush at Croke Park. The crowd had spilled out of the hospital and into the street, where people gathered on the pavement. A few people recognized Sean and knew about Con having been shot, so they made way for him as he led us into the hospital. We followed him up the stairs and headed for the wards, but found our way barred by one of the nursing nuns.

"You cannot come in," she said firmly.

"My brother's in there," said Uncle Sean. "This woman's husband. And this is his son."

"There are lots of husbands and brothers and sons in here today," she said. "The doctors need space and time to treat them. They can't do that if the ward is full of their relatives."

Just then, a doctor appeared from the ward.

"What's going on here?" he demanded.

"My name is Sean Donnelly," said Uncle Sean. "I brought my brother, Con, in earlier. He was injured at Croke Park. This is his wife and son to see him."

The doctor turned to Aunt Kathleen. "Mrs Donnelly, your husband is alive, but we are still working on him."

"What does that mean?" asked Kathleen.

"Luckily for him, the bullet struck on the right side of his chest rather than the left, missing his heart. But the bullet went through the top of his lung. At the moment he's unconscious and we are working to stabilize him. But if you wait downstairs, we'll tell you when he's ready to be seen."

The doctor then turned to Sean.

"Mr Donnelly, can I have a word with you?"

Aunt Kathleen looked as if she was going to protest at being cut out, but Aunt Mary held her back as the doctor led Uncle Sean to one side. I moved as near as I could to try and hear what was being said.

"Mr Donnelly, your brother was shot," said the doctor in a low voice.

"Yes, that's why he's here," said Uncle Sean curtly.

"I meant earlier today, before the events of Croke Park," said the doctor. "That wound on his arm. It's a bullet wound."

Sean looked at the doctor warily, and I felt a stab of panic. The doctor knew! He'd worked out that Con had been involved in this morning's shootings! Was he going to report Con? If so, he'd be hanged for sure.

Sean looked the doctor squarely in the face and asked in a whisper: "And if it is a bullet wound. So what?"

The doctor gave a shrug.

"Then whoever sewed it up did a very good job. He could train as a doctor."

She! I wanted to shout out. *My Aunt Mary sewed him up!* But I kept quiet, just listened as the doctor continued.

"We'll do our best for him. Luckily he's young and strong, which is in his favour. But when he's discharged from hospital, tell him to be more careful in future."

With that, the doctor held out his hand and Sean shook it.

"We'll do our best for your brother, Mr Donnelly," said the doctor.

Then he went back onto the ward.

CHAPTER

After the doctor had gone, Aunt Kathleen rushed over to Uncle Sean.

"What did he say?" she demanded.

"He said that Con's young and strong. The doctor thinks he'll be all right once they've patched him up."

"Well, that's a relief," said Aunt Mary. "I suppose since he's not awake yet there's no need for all of us to be here. I'll stay with Kathleen while you take the boys home, Sean."

Rory, Sean and I said goodbye and drove back home

in the taxi. It was late and poor Rory was worn out with all that had happened so Sean put him to sleep in my bed as soon as we got in. Then we went into the kitchen and Sean put the kettle on for a cup of tea, and he made us each a sandwich.

We sat at the kitchen table with our sandwiches and tea in silence, both of us thinking of Con lying in the hospital, and everything that had happened during this dreadful and terrifying day. All the dead and badly wounded.

"We've never really talked about what happened at the Easter Rising, Liam," said Uncle Sean suddenly. "You were young when it happened and as time passed, I didn't like to think about it. About that time."

"I know Da was killed at the rising," I said. I hesitated, then added: "You said it was because there weren't enough men to fight with him and the others."

Sean nodded. "Liam, after what happened today, this isn't going to end. The struggle for Irish freedom will be your struggle when you get older, and – God forbid – your children's. So it's important you listen to what I say to you today.

"The downfall of the Irish is that we have good and

brave intentions, but they get messed up by different groups fighting one another rather than fighting our common enemy, the British.

"The Easter Rising is a good example. In 1916, the IRA was made of two different organizations, The Irish Republican Brotherhood and the Irish Volunteers. The IRB thought that while Britain was at war with Germany it was a good time for we Irish to rise up and kick the British out. The British had enough to deal with over the war in Germany, so their forces would be smaller.

"The problem was there were big divisions between the IRB and the Irish Volunteers. On one side you had Patrick Pearse, Joseph Plunkett, Thomas MacDonagh and Eamonn Ceannt, who said Easter 1916 was the ideal time for the rising to happen.

"But there were others, mainly Eeoin MacNeil and Denis McCullough – the leaders of the Volunteers – who said the attack should only go ahead if it was guaranteed it would succeed. For that to happen they needed the supply of weapons and ammunition that had been promised by Germany – twenty thousand rifles and a million rounds of ammunition.

"But the weapons never arrived. The British found out about the supplies and intercepted the ship they were being brought in on. The fact that the weapons and ammunition were heading for Ireland alerted the British to the fact that something big was about to happen, so they increased their security.

"Pearse, Plunkett and the others said the rising should go ahead anyway. They felt they had a strong force of willing men and women and they were sure that once it began, others would flock to join them. But O'Neill and his side said there should be no rebellion and they issued orders to the Volunteers telling them the rising had been cancelled.

"Some Volunteers joined the rising, but many others didn't because of the orders from O'Neill. So, instead of there being tens of thousands of Irish fighters taking on the British in the rising, in Dublin there were only about one thousand two hundred and fifty. There were other risings elsewhere, in Cork and Meath and other places, with another two thousand or so. But again, because the men got contradictory orders, with the leaders of the Volunteers telling them the rising had been cancelled, it all petered out."

"Da was killed at the General Post Office," I said.

"He was," said Sean. "He died fighting bravely. The General Post Office was the first place taken and became the rebels' headquarters. There were other key places taken where the rebels held out – South Dublin Union, Jacob's Biscuit Factory … but the General Post Office was the main place. The British shelled it, day after day. When it became obvious to Pearse that the longer it went on the more Irish people would die, he did what he had to do and surrendered."

Sean shook his head. "The rising lasted five days, but it was sixteen thousand British troops and one thousand armed police against the Irish fighters," he said sadly. "To this day I wonder if the outcome would have been different if the Volunteers hadn't been told the rising had been cancelled. If there had been more men fighting."

Suddenly there was a knock at the door, startling us both.

"Who is it?" Uncle Sean called out.

"Tom Flanagan," came the reply.

Sean opened the door. It was the man who'd been in the kitchen at the house in Lower Gardiner Street.

He saw me and nodded in greeting, but there was no smile this time. His face wore a grim expression.

"I heard about Con," he said to Sean.

"He's at the hospital," replied Sean.

"Yes, so I heard," said Tom. "I came to tell you the news about Dick McKee and Peadar Clancy. You know they were taken to Dublin Castle?"

"With the man from Clare, Conor Clune." Sean nodded.

"They were shot this evening," said Tom. "By the Tans who were holding them. They claimed the three of them grabbed guns and hand grenades and tried to escape, so they were shot dead. But as they were locked in, I can't see how that could be true. The word is it was revenge for what happened this morning, the shooting of the Cairo Gang."

"Were they questioned by the Tans before they were killed?" asked Sean.

"They were, but by all accounts they gave no names," said Tom. "But, just in case, be on your guard, Sean. And tell Con the same."

He shook hands with Sean, then with me.

"Make sure you take care of them, Liam," he said.

He opened the door and left. Sean rebolted the door. I followed him back to the kitchen.

"Three more dead martyrs for Ireland," he said bitterly as he sat down at the table. "And there'll be many more before this war is over."

Aunt Mary and Aunt Kathleen returned home as dawn was breaking the next morning.

"Con woke up a couple of hours after you left," said Aunt Mary. "He'll need to stay in hospital for a while, but he's pulled through the worst of it." She gave Sean a stern look. "But there'll be no more of what happened," she told him.

"But, Mary—" began Sean.

"Freedom for Ireland will come," said Mary. "But we don't need all the men in our family to die for it. You did your part. Let others do theirs. It needn't cost the blood of all."

EPILOGUE

A week later Con left hospital and returned home. On that same day, 28th November, in west Cork, an IRA unit ambushed a patrol of Tans and killed all but one of them. The war got worse, not just in Dublin but across the whole of Ireland. The county of Cork seemed to be singled out by the Tans for revenge attacks. They burnt part of the town of Middleton in Cork, and then burnt the centre of the city of Cork itself. Even worse, the Tans shot at the firemen who were sent to put out the blaze.

The year 1921 was worse than any that had come before, with more people killed during the first six months than in the whole of the previous three years.

Peace, of a sort, finally came in July 1921, when a truce was declared. The truce was followed by talks between the British Government and our own elected Irish Government, which the British at last recognized.

I remember us getting the news in our street, and Aunt Mary going to church to give thanks for there being peace at last. But it was not to be.

The talks between the British and Irish representatives dragged on. Michael Collins and his party brought back an agreement from London for an Irish Free State, which Collins said was a stepping stone towards full independence. However, the agreement didn't include the province of Ulster. Eamon de Valera and others claimed that Collins had betrayed Ireland by not insisting on full independence for all of Ireland, including Ulster.

It seemed to me it was just as Uncle Sean had said: the Irish have good and brave intentions, but they get messed up by different groups fighting one another rather than fighting our common enemy.

Civil War came to Ireland. Those who supported Michael Collins against those who backed Eamon de Valera. And after all that had gone before, Uncle Sean was shot dead, not by a Tan or a British soldier, but by another Irish Republican.

But that's another story.

HISTORICAL NOTE:

THE IRISH WAR OF INDEPENDENCE

THE PEOPLE

Liam and his family are fictitious, but their experiences are based on historical accounts of people who were involved in the struggle for Irish independence in the early 20th century and those who were caught up in the "Bloody Sunday" shootings at Croke Park. Michael Collins, Cathal Brugha, Dick McKee, Peadar Clancy, Conor Clune and the other referenced leaders of the Easter Rising were real people, and their characterizations are based on written testimonies of this time in history.

THE IRISH STRUGGLE FOR INDEPENDENCE

1169–1171: Ireland was brought under English governance through a series of invasions.

1558–1625: In order to consolidate Protestant power after Henry VIII's separation from the Catholic Church, Elizabeth I and James VI granted land in Ireland to Protestant English gentry. This took power away from the largely Catholic Irish population.

1649: Oliver Cromwell launched a military campaign against Ireland, following an Irish rebellion against English rule. Cromwell's bloodthirsty campaign lasted until 1653.

1776: Ireland, although still mainly Catholic, was now dominated by English Protestant rule. In 1641, Catholics had owned 60 per cent of the land in Ireland, but by 1776, Catholics owned just 5 per cent of the land.

1801: The Act of Union passed, by which Ireland became part of the United Kingdom of Great Britain and Ireland.

1801–1870: A campaign, led by Irish MPs in the British

parliament, demanded that the citizens of Ireland had the right to rule themselves as an independent nation. This was known as Home Rule. From 1870 there were many attempts to pass a Home Rule for Ireland bill in the British Parliament, but all failed.

1913: The Irish Volunteers was formed, who – if they couldn't gain independence by political means – were determined to gain it by an armed uprising.

1916: The Easter Rising began in Dublin when a force of Irish Volunteers led by Patrick Pearse, James Connolly and others rose up in armed rebellion to try to overthrow British rule. The rebellion was crushed and the leaders were executed. Others were arrested and sentenced to death, but their sentences commuted to imprisonment. Almost two thousand of those were imprisoned at Frongoch internment camp in Wales. They included Michael Collins, the military commander of the Volunteers.

1917: An Assembly of Irish Volunteers took place in Dublin to elect their leaders. Eamon de Valera was elected President, Michael Collins was elected Director of Organisation and Cathal Brugha was elected Chairman.

1918: During the British election, mostly Sinn Féin candidates were elected in Ireland. They refused to take their seats in Westminster, as they refused to recognize the authority of the British Parliament over Ireland. Instead they formed an Irish Government in Ireland, with Eamon de Valera as President, along with Michael Collins and Cathal Brugha in senior government positions.

21 January 1919: The first Dáil Éireann (Government of the Irish Republic) was held in Dublin. British authorities declared the Dail illegal.

1919: Irish War of Independence begins.

1920: The Irish Volunteers were renamed the IRA (Irish Republican Army), led by Michael Collins.

11 July 1921:   A truce was declared between Britain and Ireland. This was instigated by the British Prime Minister, David Lloyd George. With de Valera as president of the newly formed Irish Republic, talks began with the British Government who intended to grant Ireland a form of Home Rule. Southern Ireland would be the Irish Free State, but would still be part of the British Empire, with Northern Ireland (Ulster) remaining part of Britain. Some IRA leaders, led by Michael Collins, agreed to the terms of this treaty. Others, led by President Eamon de Valera, opposed it, insisting that Ireland needed to remain united and be independent of Britain. This led to the Irish Civil War (June 1922 to May 1923) in which more Irish people died than during the War of Independence.

BLOODY SUNDAY

Saturday, 20th November 1920

On the evening of Saturday 20th November there was a meeting of Dublin IRA members at which the assassination teams were briefed on their targets. Collins' plan had been to kill fifty British intelligence officers and informers, but the list was reduced to thirty-five at the insistence of Cathal Brugha (Minister for Defence in the rebel Irish Government) on the grounds that there was insufficient evidence against some of the men.

After the meeting had ended, Collins and others went to Vaughan's Hotel, Parnell Square. There, they were met by Conor Clune – an IRA Volunteer from County Clare. While they were in the hotel, a porter became suspicious of one of the guests who'd made a late-night telephone call and then left the hotel. He warned the IRA men, who quickly left the building. The hotel was raided shortly after. Everyone got away – except Conor Clune.

A few hours later, McKee and Clancy were arrested in Sean Fitzpatrick's of Gloucester Street and taken to

Dublin Castle. It was later discovered that they had been betrayed to the British authorities by an ex-British army soldier.

Sunday 21st November 1920
Morning

Early in the morning, the IRA assassination teams went into action in Dublin. At 28 Upper Pembroke Street, two army officers were killed and a third officer was wounded in the attack. He later died of his injuries.

At 38 Upper Mount Street, two intelligence officers were killed.

At 22 Lower Mount Street, one intelligence officer was killed and another escaped. The building was then surrounded by Black and Tans and the IRA team was forced to shoot its way out. One IRA man, Frank Teeling, was wounded and captured. Two Black and Tans – who had been sent to bring reinforcements – were captured and killed by the IRA. At 117 Morehampton Road, the IRA killed an intelligence officer, but also shot the civilian landlord, presumably by mistake. At the Gresham Hotel, the IRA killed another civilian, Patrick McCormack, along with another man, Leonard Wilde, who was suspected of being an intelligence officer. At 119 Lower Baggot Street, the British army officer Captain G. T. Baggallay was killed by the IRA.

Afternoon

Dublin were scheduled to play Tipperary at Croke Park in the GAA football final, due to start at 2.45 p.m. The match – watched by a crowd of five thousand – began thirty minutes late at 3.15 p.m. British security forces were sent to raid the match in an attempt to arrest the people who'd carried out the killings that morning. Their orders were to surround the ground, guard the exits and search every man in Croke Park.

The convoy arrived at 3.25 p.m. The Black and Tans in the leading vehicles jumped out and ran down the passage to the canal end gate. However, instead of ordering the crowd to leave and be searched, they forced their way through the turnstiles and started firing with revolvers and rifles. According to a report in Irish newspaper, the *Freeman's Journal*:

"The spectators were startled by a volley of shots

fired from inside the turnstile entrances. Armed and uniformed men were seen entering the field, and immediately after the firing broke out scenes of the wildest confusion took place. The spectators made a rush for the far side of Croke Park and shots were fired over their heads and into the crowd."

Their commander, Major Mills, later admitted that his men were "excited and out of hand". At the other end of Croke Park, the soldiers on Clonliffe Road were startled by the sound of gunfire and the sight of panicked people fleeing the grounds. As the spectators streamed out, an armoured car on St James Avenue fired its machine gun over the heads of the crowd, trying to halt them.

By the time Major Mills had got his men back under control, seven people had been shot dead, and five more fatally wounded. Another two had been trampled to death in the stampede. Fourteen people died in total and an additional sixty to seventy civilians were injured.

Two football players, Michael Hogan and Jim Egan, were shot. Hogan was killed, but Egan survived. The dead included Jeannie Boyle, who had gone to the match with her fiancée, and was due to be married five days later. Two boys, Jerome O'Leary, aged ten, and William Robinson, aged eleven were also killed. The Black and Tans suffered no casualties.

After the event, to try and justify the action, the British authorities in Dublin Castle – which was the regional seat of British Government in Ireland – released a press statement which said:

"A number of men came to Dublin under the guise of attending a football match between Tipperary and Dublin; but their real intention was to take part in a series of murderous outrages. Learning that a number of these gunmen were present in Croke Park, the Crown forces went to raid the field. It was the original intention that an officer would go to the centre of the field and speak from a megaphone, inviting the assassins to come forward. But on their approach, armed guards gave warning. Shots were fired to warn the wanted men, who caused a stampede and escaped in the confusion."

Many publications, including *The Times*, ridiculed this version of events. The British Brigadier Frank Percy Crozier, technically in command that day, resigned over the unjustified actions of the men under his command. One of Crozier's officers told him that, "Black and Tans fired into the crowd without any provocation whatsoever."

IF YOU ENJOYED

INDEPENDENCE
WAR IN IRELAND, 20–21 NOVEMBER 1920

READ ON FOR A TASTE OF

PLAGUE
OUTBREAK IN LONDON, 1665–1666

CHAPTER

It was late in the evening and I was about to say goodbye to my mother for the very last time. The moment had come for me to try and escape, and I knew that once I left our house I would probably never see her again – not in this life, anyway.

"Are you sure you have everything you need, Daniel?" she whispered. "We should try to fit a warm undershirt into your satchel and some more food."

We were standing in my father's workshop on the ground floor of our house. Mother was holding a candle, its tiny yellow flame pushing the shadows into the corners, the light glinting off the tools scattered on the floor where Father had dropped them. She was wearing a white nightgown and her face was deathly pale, with dark smudges under her eyes. Her black hair hung loose to her shoulders, but I could still see the bruised, painful swellings on both sides of her neck.

I knew she felt really ill and that she was only keeping herself going for my sake. She had spent the previous hour – our final precious moments together – packing my satchel and giving me advice. I stood there in my best jacket and breeches, wearing the stockings she had knitted for me and the shoes she had often polished. I clutched the satchel, feeling as if the world was coming to an end.

"Please, Mother, don't make me do this," I said. I was whispering too and my voice trembled. A tear slid down my cheek. "Let me stay here with you."

I stepped forwards to throw my arms round her, but she quickly backed away. She held up her hands to stop me touching her. "You know that can't be, Daniel," she said. "It's a miracle that you haven't already fallen ill. I hate making you leave, but as God is my witness, I won't let you stay, however much you plead. Your only chance is to escape tonight, before the sickness takes you, as it took your father and brothers."

I had already said goodbye to them. My older brothers William and Henry lay dead on their beds upstairs, their necks swollen like Mother's. Father lay cold and stiff on the bed he had shared with Mother for as long as I could remember, the one in which I had been born. He had been the first to fall ill, collapsing in his workshop three days ago. Although it felt like a hundred years of grief and sorrow had passed since then.

"But it's not right," I said. "I would rather stay here and die than leave you!"

"Hush now," she said, her voice gentle. "I'll be with you forever, wherever you are. All you have to do is listen to your heart and you will hear my voice."

I tried arguing with her. I fell to my knees and begged her to let me stay, but she refused to listen, even though she was crying too, the tears dripping off her cheeks. She would not change her mind.

Father had often said, "By heaven, Meg, you can be so stubborn!" He had always said it with a loving smile, though. We had been a happy family.

When I was young, life had been tough under the rule of the Puritans, but in 1660 we'd got a new king, King Charles II. The next few years were good – for the country, for London and for my family. Lots of new houses were built, and as Father was a good carpenter, his business had prospered. The Puritans had banned bright clothes, but now everyone wanted them, and Mother was a fine seamstress, so she was soon earning us extra money. My brothers worked with Father, but Mother wanted me to learn to read and write. She sent me to a school in Milk Street, where I did well. Before long, I was reading and writing letters for Father – I loved helping him.

I also loved living in London – it was a wonderful place at that time. I roamed all over the city, from the great houses of the rich on the Strand by the river Thames to the hovels of St Giles beyond the northern wall, and from old St Paul's cathedral on Ludgate Hill in the West to the forbidding castle battlements of the Tower of London in the East. The streets were always busy, full of noise and colour, people buying and selling, talking and arguing. Father told me London was the biggest city in the country by far, with more people in it than pebbles on the banks of the Thames.

Then things started to go wrong. We began hearing rumours about people dying from the plague. It didn't bother us to begin with. The plague had first struck hundreds of years ago, when it was called the Black Death, and it had never really gone away. Every year there were a few plague deaths in the hovels of St Giles to the north-west of the city, but that was where it usually stayed.

Then the number of dead started to rise, as everyone could see in the Bills of Mortality the Lord Mayor ordered to be pasted up everywhere. Last winter, in the early part of 1665, when the weather was cold, the deaths were still in single figures and still mostly confined to St Giles. By the spring, however, it was fifty a week in some parishes and by the summer it was hundreds. It was worst in the poor parts of the city, but no one was truly safe. The rich died too, as did the middling sort of people – like my family.

Many people fled the city and for a while the streets were choked with coaches and carts, with columns of frightened people trudging along beside them. The king left the great Palace of Whitehall with his family and went up the Thames to his other fine home at Hampton Court. But lots of families, including my own, had nowhere to go outside London. Father also said we couldn't abandon our home and leave it unguarded. Thieves would break in as soon as they saw we were gone and they would steal everything we owned.

So we stayed and tried to carry on as before, although that wasn't really possible. Men went round the streets with carts – people called them the dead carts – yelling, "Bring out your dead!" and collecting the bodies of all those who had passed away. London is a city full of churches and their bells rang constantly for the endless funerals. Before long there was no space left in the cemeteries, so the Lord Mayor ordered that enormous pits should be dug for the bodies, both inside the city and beyond the walls.

Some people thought the plague, known as the pestilence, was spread by stray cats, so the Lord

Mayor ordered all cats to be killed. But the cats had kept the rats under control and soon there were rats everywhere. The taverns were packed with people trying to have fun in the short time they might have left or making sure they got so drunk they didn't think about death. The churches were also packed with people praying to God to save them and their families.

The plague finally reached our street, Bear Alley, in early June. Within a week most of the doors bore red crosses. When one appeared on the house next to ours, we spent the whole night on our knees praying. I wasn't sure how much good our prayers would do. I didn't say that, of course. How could I, when Father prayed every morning in a loud voice and read us passages from the Bible to give us strength? His favourite was Psalm 23, the one that includes the lines: *Yea, though I walk through the valley of the shadow of death, I will fear no evil: for thou art with me; thy rod and thy staff they comfort me.*

Both my parents had always been strong in their faith. I couldn't let them know that I was confused and wondering if God even cared. As I stood there with my mother on that last night, I knew that her faith in God was all she had left. . .

Suddenly, we heard a familiar loud *BONG!* sounding over the streets outside. It echoed off the houses and was swiftly followed by another and another. The great bells of old St Paul's Cathedral were being rung to let the city know that it was midnight. Mother and I froze and stared at each other. Then she stepped past me and opened the small window in the workshop's far wall.

"We must hurry!" she hissed, fear and panic in her face. "I hadn't realized it was so late. We're running out of time … the watchman will be back soon!"

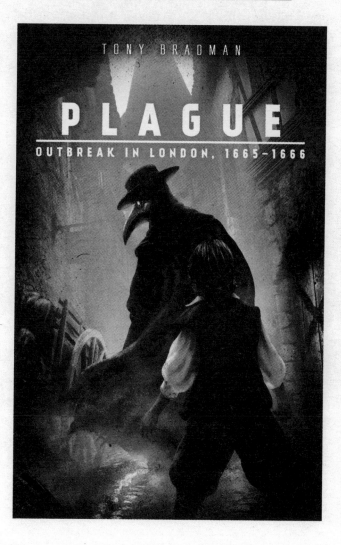

A GRIPPING FIRST-HAND
ACCOUNT OF ONE OF THE MOST
DANGEROUS TIMES IN HISTORY

TONY BRADMAN

PLAGUE

OUTBREAK IN LONDON, 1665-1666